To Joan, who performs feats of wonder.
— **T.L.**

For every teacher,
thank you for encouraging me to dream.
— **M.C.**

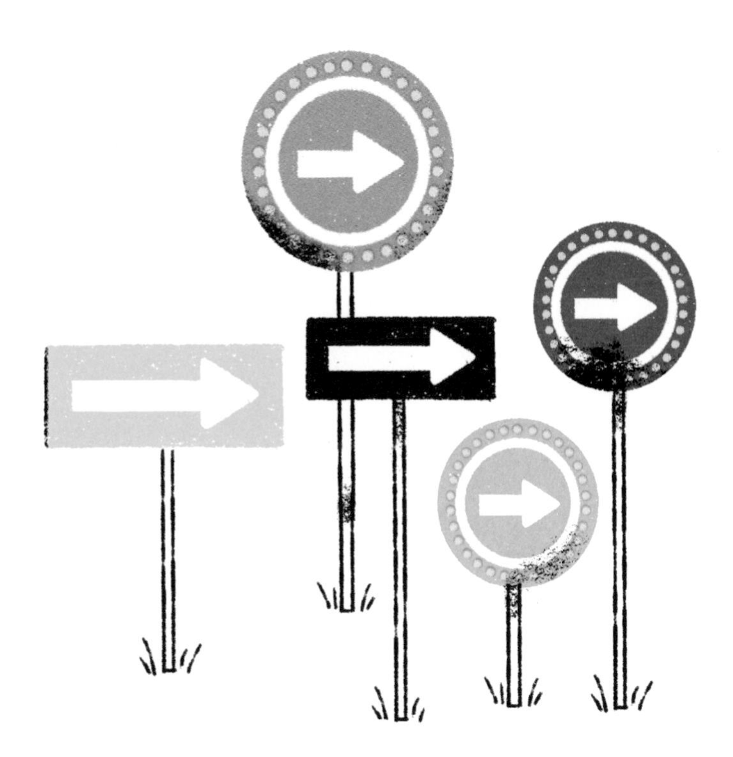

Tundra Books, an imprint of Penguin Random House Canada Young Readers,
a Penguin Random House Company

Lazar, Tara, author
Your first day of circus school / Tara Lazar ; illustrated
by Melissa Crowton.

Issued also in print and electronic formats.
ISBN 978-0-7352-6371-0 (hardcover).—ISBN 978-0-7352-6372-7 (EPUB)

I. Crowton, Melissa, illustrator II. Title.

PZ7.L42Yo 2019 j813'.6 C2018-903158-1
C2018-903159-X

Published simultaneously in the United States of America by Tundra Books of Northern New York, an imprint of Penguin Random House Canada Young Readers, a Penguin Random House Company

Library of Congress Control Number: 2018946082

Edited by Peter Phillips and Samantha Swenson
Designed by John Martz
The artwork in this book was created digitally.
The text was set in Cabrito Inverto.

Printed and bound in China

www.penguinrandomhouse.ca

1 2 3 4 5 23 22 21 20 19

Penguin
Random House
TUNDRA BOOKS

YOUR FIRST DAY OF CIRCUS SCHOOL

TARA LAZAR

ILLUSTRATED BY
MELISSA CROWTON

Ladies and gentlemen, boys and girls of all ages!
It's the most amazing day on earth:

YOUR FIRST DAY OF SCHOOL!

Who can sleep before
the big day?

You're probably tired
this morning and
dragging your feet.

Make sure you
find a uniform
that fits.

Take time to eat a balanced breakfast . . .

and don't forget to pack a snack.

Don't worry, the bus has an **ENDLESS** number of seats!

Welcome one and all!

STEP RIGHT UP!

School looks

BIG!

But you'll
find your way
around.

WALK THIS WAY!

Your big brother will
show you the ropes.

Don't let the kids in the **HIGHER GRADES** run you over.

You'll make lots of new friends if you put on a **SMILE.**

Once you find your class,
try not to sit behind
the tall kid.

And it's important to
learn your teacher's name.

I bet you've worked up
quite an appetite.

Watch out. The cafeteria
can be a real **ZOO**.

You can let off some
STEAM during recess . . .

but watch out for other stuff that steams!

I know it's
a lot to
JUGGLE
on your
first day.

And you probably have **HIGH** expectations.

But you'll find a way to
rise above it all . . .

and soar through the air
with the greatest of ease.

Well, look at that.

You're a fast
learner, kiddo.

At the **TOP** of the class already!

After all, you're just like
your big brother . . .

in so many ways.

Was your first day awesome?

I hope you had a **BLAST!**

I bet you can't wait until tomorrow.
And the day after. And the day after that!

Your big brother will be there to cheer you on every step of the way.